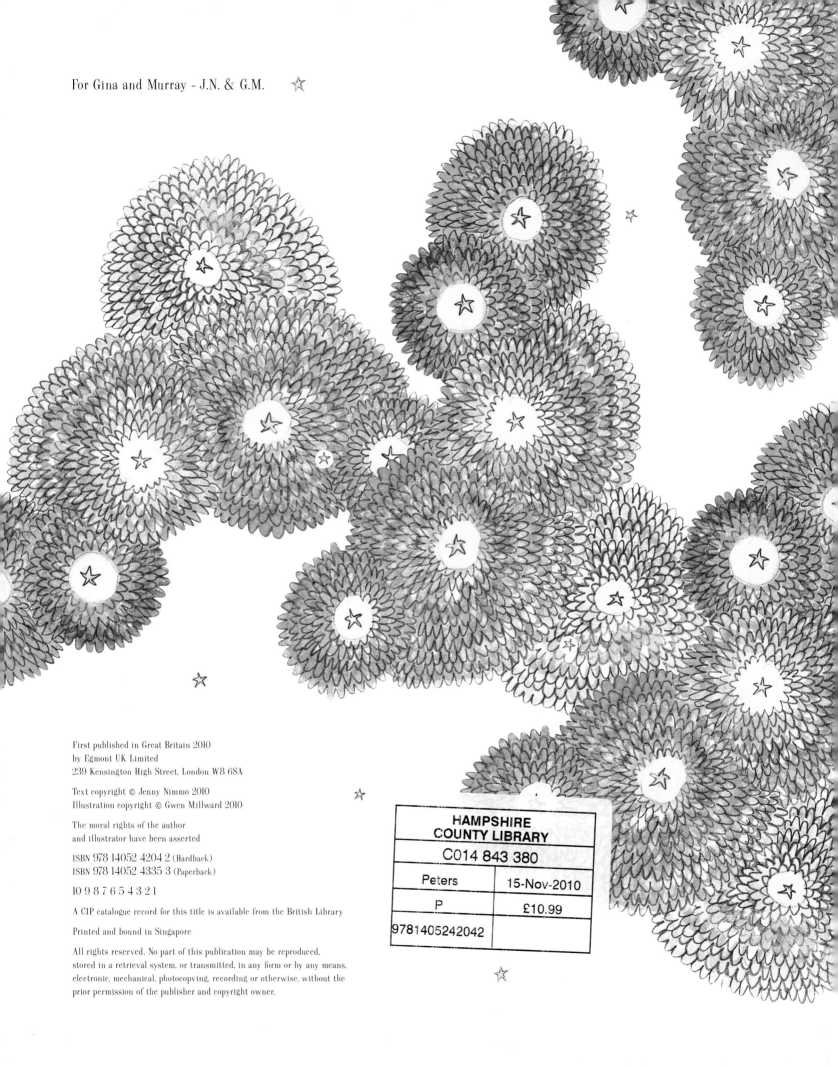

For Gina and Murray - J.N. & G.M.

First published in Great Britain 2010
by Egmont UK Limited
239 Kensington High Street, London W8 6SA

Text copyright © Jenny Nimmo 2010
Illustration copyright © Gwen Millward 2010

The moral rights of the author
and illustrator have been asserted

ISBN 978 14052 4204 2 (Hardback)
ISBN 978 14052 4335 3 (Paperback)

10 9 8 7 6 5 4 3 2 1

A CIP catalogue record for this title is available from the British Library

Printed and bound in Singapore

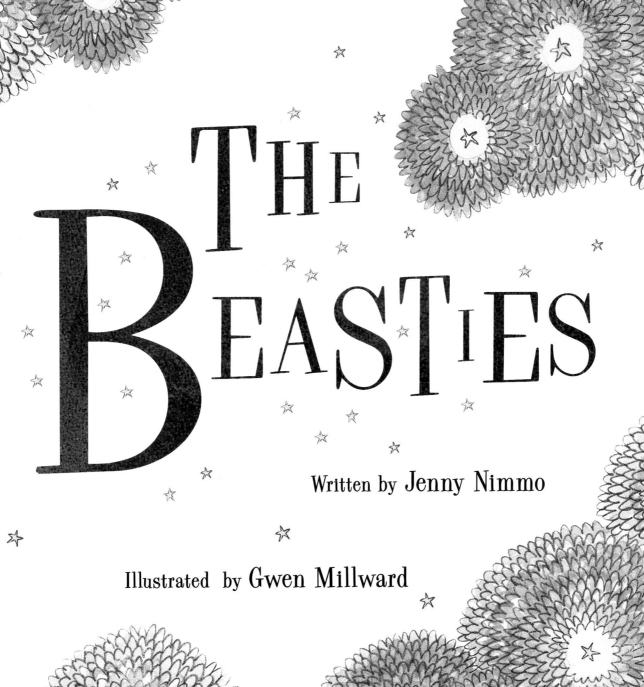

THE BEASTIES

Written by Jenny Nimmo

Illustrated by Gwen Millward

The **Beasties** came to Daisy's house
on a night when she couldn't sleep.

Her new room was too strange
and her new bed was too big.

As she lay awake, listening to
the sounds in the street . . .

Daisy thought hard. Then she said, slowly,
'This shell belonged to a mermaid...'

'Where was the mermaid?'
asked the Beasties.

Daisy thought hard again.
'She was in the sea, and the shell
was in her hair. She was crying because
she was caught in a net.

And ... and so I jumped onto a rock.
I nearly fell but I took her hand ...
and pulled her out.

At first the shell
looked very ordinary.

But then she put it to her ear

and heard the sea . . .

'I won't,' **said Daisy.** 'But, please, can I have another story?'

Floot looked thoughtful.

'I think you can tell your own story,' he said, and he held out a shell.

'All by myself?'
Daisy wasn't sure.

'And I'm Ferdinand,' growled the last.
'Don't tell anyone
you've seen us!'

The Beasties!

Daisy opened her mouth to scream.

But she didn't, because . . .
the Beasties were very, very small.

'Don't be afraid,' said one.
'We're storytellers.
My name
is Weevil.'

'I'm Floot,'
piped the next Beastie.

Books

Toys

Daisy's diary

very slowly,

looked her bed . . .
under

and saw . . .

Daisy was really brave.

She put on her bedside light and slowly,

Something rustled. What was that?
Daisy's heart went pit-a-pat.

It wasn't a musical sound,

or a tree by the window

or a truck in the street.

'What shall we do next?'
said a growly voice.

Daisy jumped.

There was another rustle.
Where was it coming from?

The following night Daisy
lay awake, wondering if a story
would begin.
 But everything was quiet.

Daisy stared into the dark
 and cried,
 'I wish I could have a story.'

I sang the princess's favourite song
and she recognised the tune.
"I was lost," she cried,
"but now you have found me."

She gave me this button
for faithfulness.

We said goodbye to the friendly wolves
and I led my princess home.'

Daisy's eyes were already closed.
Floot's musical voice
had sung her to sleep.

'This **button** was stitched
to a princess's coat,'
piped Floot in his musical voice.

'When the princess was small,
I used to sing her to sleep.
One day, in a game of hide-and-seek,
the princess disappeared.

I searched for my princess everywhere.
I thought she was lost forever.

And then, in the forest,
one moonlit night, I saw a girl
playing with wolves.

The very next night,
as Daisy lay awake,
she heard a musical sound.

What was that?
    Daisy's heart went pit-a-pat.

Was someone whistling a tune?

No.
It sounded like . . .

. . . a story!

SHOES

Daisy closed her eyes.
She dreamed that
she was in the sky,
flying with
the beautiful bird.

But then down came my friend,
the **beautiful bird**, just in time to rescue me.
She gave me this feather for friendship.

And that's the end of my story.'

'This **feather** belonged to a beautiful bird,'
said Weevil in his clickety voice.

'When I was young I travelled
on a sailing ship.
I used to feed a beautiful bird
with crumbs from a biscuit tin.

When the ship was wrecked in a terrible storm,
the sailors escaped in their boats.

But I was left alone on a shore
where dangerous creatures lived.
They looked at me hungrily.

The very next night, as Daisy
lay awake in her big new bed,
in her strange new room,
      she heard a clicking sound.

What was that?
Daisy's heart went pit-a-pat.
Was it a tree tapping the window?

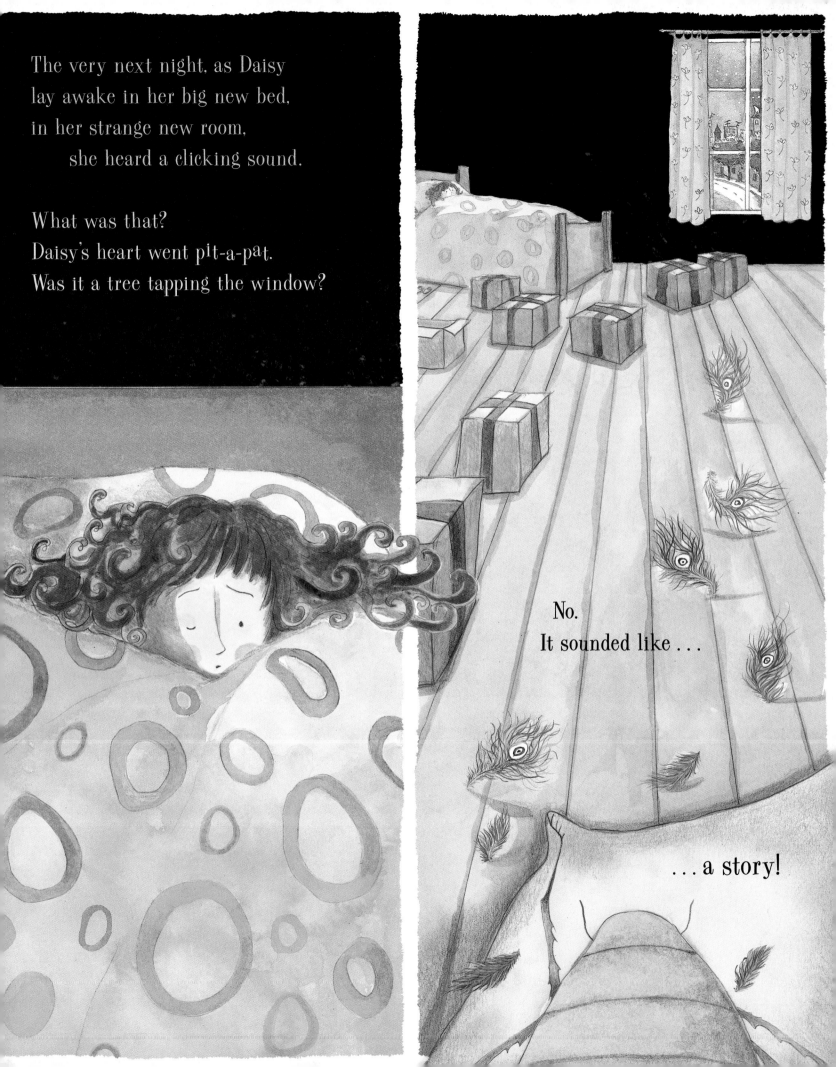

No.
It sounded like . . .

. . . a story!

Daisy wondered about that ring.
Was it gold or silver
or studded with jewels?

She wondered

and wondered until

she fell asleep.

I bared my shining teeth
and flashed my
razor-sharp claws.

With **screams** of terror,
those robbers ran
for their lives!

The faraway king was so pleased,
he gave me this ring for my bravery.

And that's the end of my story.'

'This **ring** belonged to
a faraway king,'
said Ferdinand's growly voice.

'I used to guard his treasures while he slept.
One night two robbers crept up.
They didn't see me at first.

But suddenly
I **leapt** out.

I **roared**.

I **breathed** fire.

As Daisy stared into the dark,
she heard a growly sound.

What was that?
    Daisy's heart went pit-a-pat.

        Was it a truck in the street?

TOYS

No.
It sounded like . . .

. . . a story!

She didn't see them
spread their treasures
underneath
her bed.

There were shells and buttons,
feathers and pearls,

beans and flowers,
silver and gold.

she didn't see Weevil,
Floot and Ferdinand
creep into her room.

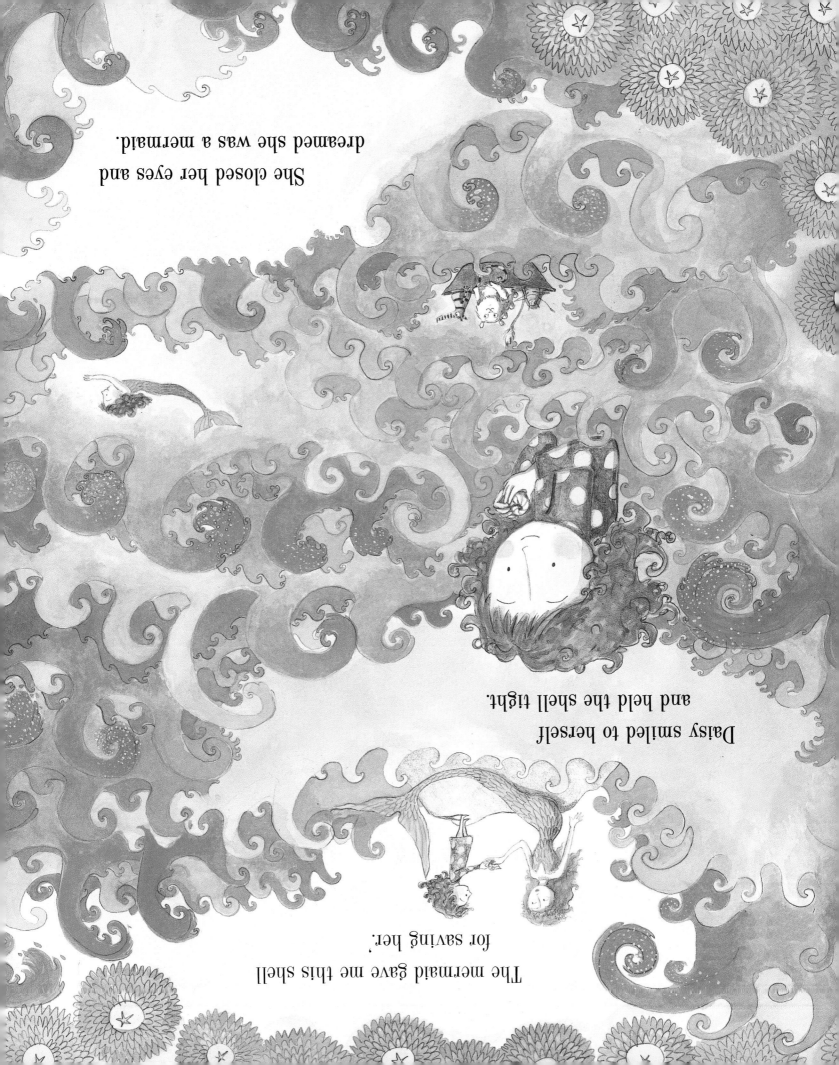

She closed her eyes and
dreamed she was a mermaid.

Daisy smiled to herself
and held the shell tight.

'The mermaid gave me this shell
for saving her.'

'Your bed won't seem so big
anymore and your room
won't seem so strange.

You can tell your
own stories now.'

And they crept out
of her room.

'Night night, Daisy!'
whispered the Beasties.